L
Christmas
Animals

STANDARD
PUBLISHING
Cincinnati, Ohio

Henrietta D. Gambill
illustrated by Kathy Parks

To John, Matthew, Kelsey, and Griffin
with love

The Standard Publishing Company, Cincinnati, Ohio
A division of Standex International Corporation
© 1994 by The Standard Publishing Company
All rights reserved.
Printed in the United States of America
01 00 99 98 97 96 95 94   5 4 3 2 1
Designed by Coleen Davis

Library of Congress Card Catalog Number 94-10000
Cataloging-in-Publication data available
ISBN 0-7847-0274-8

Little Goat lived in Nazareth, at Mary's house.
One day he heard a strange sound . . .

Swoosh! A shiny angel had appeared.
Mary was surprised!

Little Goat watched as the angel talked to Mary. *What's he telling her?* wondered Little Goat.

Little Donkey lived in a barn near Mary's house.
His mother lived there too.

One day Little Donkey saw Mary climb upon his mother's back. Joseph helped her. "Now we are ready to go to Bethlehem," said Joseph. *Why are they going to Bethlehem?* wondered Little Donkey.

Little Camel rested beside the dusty road. She was traveling to Bethlehem in a caravan of travelers and merchants.

Little Camel saw Mary
and Joseph coming
toward the caravan.

Are they going to Bethlehem with us?
wondered Little Camel.

Little Parrot sat on her perch at the Bethlehem inn, watching the travelers.

One day Little Parrot saw Mary and Joseph come to the inn. *That lady looks like she is going to have a baby* **soon,** thought Little Parrot.

Little Ox lived in the stable near the inn. He stopped munching hay when Mary and Joseph came into the stable.

Joseph began to fill a manger with clean hay.
He was in a hurry. He talked softly to Mary.
She's having a baby! Little Ox said to himself.
*Will the baby be born in **my** stable?*

Little Calf stood near Little Ox. They were friends. Little Calf and Little Ox watched as Mary put her newborn baby in the manger filled with hay. Joseph helped her. They looked happy!

Little Calf moved closer to the manger.
What's the baby's name? he wondered.

Little Lamb snuggled close to her mother on the hillside. She was *so* sleepy. She listened to the shepherds talking softly.

Suddenly a bright, shiny angel appeared! "Go to Bethlehem," the angel said. "A special baby has been born. You will find him in a manger." *What does the baby look like?* wondered Little Lamb.

Little Sheep Dog saw the angel too. Then more angels from heaven appeared in the sky. . .

. . . lots and lots of angels!
They began to praise God.
The shepherds were not afraid anymore.
"Let's go to Bethlehem," they said.
Are we going to see the baby?
wondered Little Sheep Dog.

Little Dove saw the shepherds hurrying to Bethlehem.
She flew quickly to catch up with them. They were
talking about finding a baby in a manger.

I saw a baby in a stable in Bethlehem, thought Little Dove. *Is that the baby they are going to see?*

Little Pony stood near the manger. He saw the shepherds come into the stable.

They were happy to find the baby. "An angel told us we would find baby Jesus here," they said.

Will the shepherds tell everyone that Jesus has been born? wondered Little Pony.

When the shepherds left the stable, they did tell everyone about the baby in the manger.

But all the animals wondered. Do we have to wonder too? No. Just like the shepherds, we know who he was — little baby Jesus, God's own Son.